Slacklining and Other EXTREME ROPE SPORTS

by Elliott Smith

Consultant: Daniel Lee
Outdoor Emergency Care Certified

CAPSTONE PRESS
a capstone imprint

Edge Books are published by Capstone Press
1710 Roe Crest Drive
North Mankato, Minnesota 56003
www.capstonepub.com

Library of Congress Cataloging-in-Publication Data is available on the Library of Congress website.
ISBN 978-1-5435-7322-0 (library binding)
ISBN 978-1-5435-7328-2 (ebook pdf)

Editorial Credits

Anna Butzer, editor; Cynthia Della-Rovere, designer; Kelly Garvin, media researcher; Katy LaVigne, production specialist

Photo Credits
Alamy: Helmut Meyer zur Kapellen/imageBROKER, 29, Jared Mark Alden/Aurora Photos, 17, Vitor Marigo/Aurora Photos, 15; Getty Images/Jared Alden/Aurora, 13; iStockphoto, Adventure_Photo, 23, fotografixx, 27, kasto80, 20-21, MichaelSvoboda, cover, back cover, zapatisthack, 11; Photo by Levi Allen of Leftcoast Media House, 7; Shutterstock: Fen Kuntz, 4-5, IgorSolovey, 8 (top), 19, Kevin Wells Photography, 12 (t), Myvisuals, 9, Ramb, 8 (bottom), Vitalii Nesterchuk, 24, yanik88, 12 (b)
Design elements: Shutterstock: pupsy, slavapolo

All internet sites appearing in back matter were available and accurate when this book was sent to press.

Printed and bound in the USA.
PA70

Table of Contents

CHAPTER 1

Defying Gravity

On November 13, 2017, Mia Noblet stood at the edge of the cliff of the Castleton Tower in Utah. Just one year earlier, she had watched a video of a French athlete crossing the valley on a slackline. Now it was her turn. She was going to walk across a 2-inch (5-centimeter) piece of nylon material for 1,617 feet (493 meters). Noblet placed the slackline nearly 400 feet (122 m) off the ground, with the majestic canyon all around.

"As soon as you stand up, the concentration it takes to walk is very high," Noblet recalls. "I was very focused on getting to the other side without falling."

The Castleton Tower in Moab, Utah, reaches an elevation of 6,656 feet (2,029 m).

When Noblet made it across, she collapsed to the ground in joy. The walk is one of several records the Canadian athlete has broken in her career. But Noblet's main reason for slacklining is simple: she loves having fun in the outdoors and experiencing natural beauty.

"I find great enjoyment in walking the line," she says. "When I get to the end, I'm happy. It feels like you've finished something you set out to do."

Mia Noblet highlining from the Castleton Tower to The Rectory.

CHAPTER 2

What Is Slacklining?

Sometimes the simplest ideas can lead to maximum fun. That's true of slacklining. Slacklining is a sport in which athletes walk across rope-like nylon fabric connected to two anchors. Anchors are usually a combination of ropes and hooks attached to trees or rocks. Even though it may sound like walking a tightrope, there are some differences. Athletes walk across a piece of nylon **webbing** instead of a steel cable. The fabric webbing makes the line flexible, creating a bouncy feel instead of a tight one. The webbing is also flat. This helps prevent athletes' feet from rolling off the slackline while walking.

webbing—a strong fabric, often used in place of a rope

Slacklining is about balance and control. The best slackliners can balance on a 2-inch (5-cm) piece of webbing and move with confidence. The height of slacklines can range from just a few feet off the ground to hundreds of feet in the air. Some slacklines stretch as far as 300 feet (91 m). That's about the size of a football field!

Beginners must first learn to slackline on webbing that's low to the ground.

There are several basic steps for a successful slackline walk. Athletes keep their arms extended for balance. They take small steps and try not to look down at their feet. Some slackliners prefer going barefoot to help grip the line. Others prefer sneakers, which can help when making turns and spins.

The sport of slacklining began in the 1980s. A couple of young rock climbers began practicing walking across various ropes and wires. They settled on nylon webbing and soon set up a line at their college. Before long, they went to California's Yosemite National Park to try it amongst the trees and rocks.

An athlete uses his arms to balance while slacklining over the Verdon Gorges in France.

Since then, slacklining has increased in popularity. There are places to try it across the country. The Santa Monica Pier in California recently opened a slackline park for beginners and experts. Athletes have pushed the sport to the extreme by taking it into several different directions.

Visual Glossary

crash pad
Using a crash pad under a slackline will help cushion any falls.

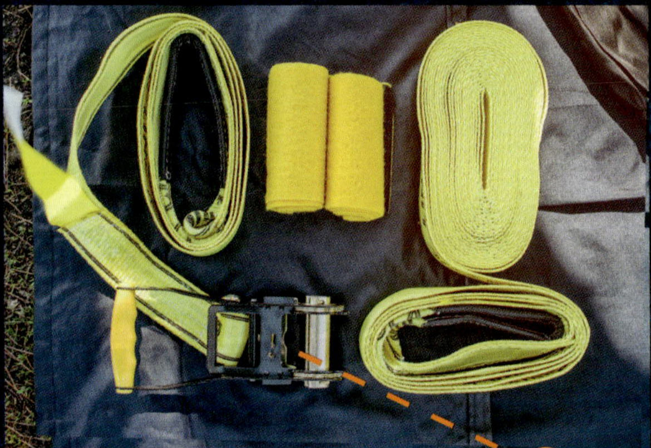

ratchet
Ratchet systems can easily be set up by one person. Ratchets have made slacklining more accessible to people.

ratchet—a device allowing motion in only one direction

climbing harness
Highliners wear a climbing harness that is connected to the leash and slackline. It will help stop a fall.
anchor
A slackline is suspended between two anchor points.
slackline
Slacklines can be made of webbing that is either stiff or stretchy. Highliners use stiffer webbing, while trickliners use webbing with some stretch.
leash
A leash is used to secure an athlete to the slackline. A leash is most important in highlining.

CHAPTER 3

Highlining

For experienced thrill-seekers, highlining combines the discipline of slacklining with the rush of heights. Highline walks are accomplished way up in the air, often at scenic locations around the globe. Safety is a big concern while highlining. Multiple anchors are **rigged** to the endpoints for protection, in case one anchor fails.

Highline athletes take extra safety precautions. They usually wear climbing harnesses or swami belts. A swami belt is a long stretch of **tubular** webbing wrapped around the climber's body. It is attached with a knot or a buckle.

rigging—the system of ropes, cables, and other equipment used to suspend a slackline
tubular—round and hollow, shaped like a tube

A highliner's leash is attached to her body and the slackline.

One of the first successful highline runs happened underneath a highway in California. The run was at 120 feet (37 m). That doesn't compare to the high **altitudes** and beautiful natural locations used now. These extreme athletes are now walking highlines at more than 1,000 feet (305 m) above ground. Mountains, the Grand Canyon, and the Eiffel Tower are some of the amazing places athletes have used for highlining. Free solo highlining is a more extreme version of the sport. Only the best athletes dare to attempt these walks and only after years and many, many hours of training. Free solo highliners do not use any kind of safety equipment, making their walks extremely dangerous.

Full of Hot Air

Highline athletes are always looking to push the boundaries of their sport. The goal is simple: to get higher than before. That is why hot air balloon highlining has become the newest test for extreme athletes. It combines two thrilling adventures in one trip!

Highliners get two hot air balloons to sail about 4,000 feet (1,219 m) above ground. The balloons are spaced apart, and a line is connected between them. The athlete then crosses the line. Athletes are not attached to the line, but they do wear parachutes in case of a fall.

The leash used in highlining should be just long enough to not get in the way while an athlete is walking.

altitude—how high a place is above sea level or Earth's surface

CHAPTER 4

Tricklining

A mix of gymnastics and trapeze artistry, tricklining is another **variation** of slacklining. The idea is to perform a series of moves, all while maintaining balance on the narrow line. The bouncy nature of the slackline makes it work almost like a trampoline. Most trickline athletes make their line tighter than a normal slackline to help with bounce. Once the line is set, it's time to do tricks!

Tricks range from simple to unbelievable. Athletes sometimes start slow, building **momentum** they use to lead into bigger moves. One simple trick is the tree, which is balancing with one foot up. A bounce walk is a series of small, quick jumps. And a drop knee is squatting down and letting one knee fall below the line. These moves are the **foundation** for bigger tricks.

variation—something that is slightly different from another thing of the same type
momentum—the amount of force in a moving object determined by the object's mass and speed
foundation—the base or basis of something

An athlete practices a drop knee move.

Extreme tricks include the squirrel backflip, where an athlete grabs their ankles while rotating in the air. A back magic has the athlete falling back onto the line, flipping, and falling back the opposite direction. And a 1080 spin is a jump with three full body turns before landing!

A trickline competition in Rio de Janeiro, Brazil in 2013

Trickline competitions are popping up around the world, where the top athletes showcase their moves. Judges score participants on a series of combos and the difficulty of their tricks. Tricks are classified in three categories. Mount and dismount are about how the athlete gets on and off the line. Contact tricks are moves during which the athlete is helped by the line. Air tricks are performed with no line contact. The best trickliners practice for years to master these moves.

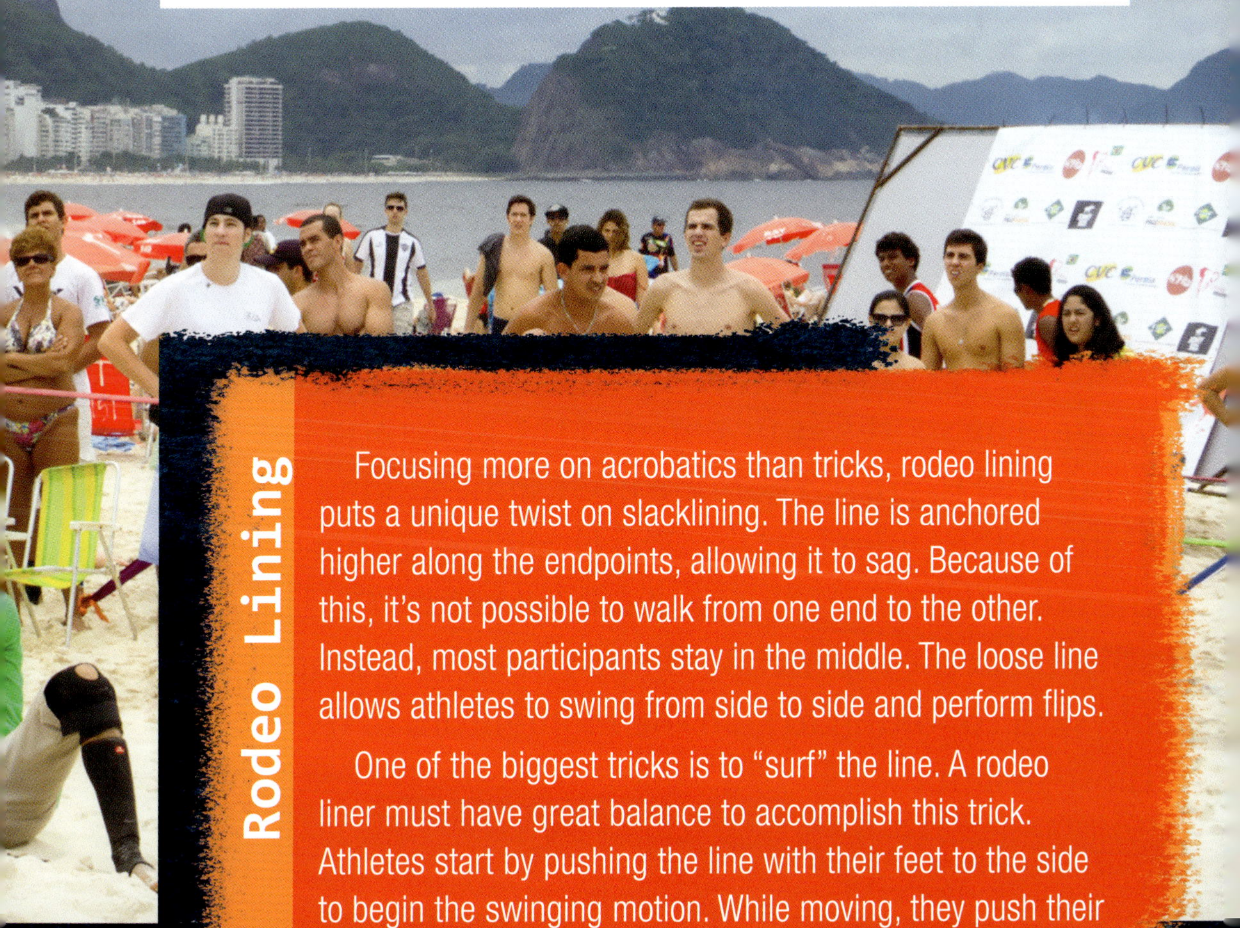

Rodeo Lining

Focusing more on acrobatics than tricks, rodeo lining puts a unique twist on slacklining. The line is anchored higher along the endpoints, allowing it to sag. Because of this, it's not possible to walk from one end to the other. Instead, most participants stay in the middle. The loose line allows athletes to swing from side to side and perform flips.

One of the biggest tricks is to "surf" the line. A rodeo liner must have great balance to accomplish this trick. Athletes start by pushing the line with their feet to the side to begin the swinging motion. While moving, they push their bodies down at the knee to build speed.

CHAPTER 5

Giant Swings

Just about everyone enjoys going to a park or playground and having fun on a swing. The feeling of flying can be thrilling. Some amusement parks have giant swing rides that **simulate** the feeling. Recently, athletes have brought the idea into the natural world.

Swings are very popular in the country of Estonia. In that country, *kiik* means swing. And the extreme sport of kiiking is swinging on a much larger scale. The goal of the sport is for athletes to **propel** themselves over the top of the swing. The sport was invented in the 1990s and has continued to grow. There are even some kiiking clubs in the United States. The challenge is that the taller the swing, the harder it is to cross the **spindle** at the top. Athletes must be in excellent physical condition to gain the momentum to reach those heights.

simulate—to give the appearance or effect of
propel—to push forward
spindle—something shaped or turned like a spindle or on which something turns

Swings used in competitions range from 15 to 20 feet (4.6 to 6.1 m) long!

Other swings are not used in competitions but give athletes a chance to see nature rushing by. The Nevis Swing in New Zealand is one of the most famous. This swing is at the edge of a mountain range. Riders travel nearly 1,100 feet (335 m) through the air with the rocky ground below.

CHAPTER 6

Rope Sports

Extreme athletes have used ropes and cords to help with their daring feats for a long time. One of the most popular rope sports remains bungee jumping. Bungee jumping is when a person jumps from a high structure while attached to an **elastic** cord. The cord stretches and then pulls the person back. While any bungee jump is exciting, some are bigger than others. The Royal Gorge Bridge in Colorado is a 1,000-foot (305-m) jump off one of the largest bridges in the country.

elastic—cord that can stretch out and return to its original size and shape

Bungee jump athletes experience four to five seconds of free falling.

Related to bungee jumping is rope jumping. Instead of a cord, these athletes use mountain climbing ropes. During a rope jump, a person slows down during the end of the fall. That allows the athlete to perform a series of flips, spins, and cartwheels on the way down. Setting up a rope jump can take months of preparation. Jumpers use a combination of ropes and **pulleys** to protect themselves during the fall. A group of athletes called the Dream Walkers are attempting a series of rope jumps around the world. Some of their planned jump locations include the Grand Canyon and the cliffs of Norway.

pulley—a grooved wheel turned by a rope, belt, or chain that often moves heavy objects

CHAPTER 7

How to Get Started

Slacklining is a great way for kids to work on their balance and stay active. Done safely and correctly, the sport can be done in a backyard or local park. There are slacklines that are specially made for beginners. These are designed to be placed low to the ground and have extra grip. Don't worry about falling! It will take time to get used to the feeling of balancing on the slackline.

"Slacklining is very simple," Mia Noblet says. "You have a line, you have yourself, and you put one foot in front of the other. There's never an age that's too young to start."

First-time slackliners should set up their slackline between knee and shoulder height.

Most beginner slacklines have a **ratchet** system which allows it to be set up low to the ground and anchored to trees. Make sure an adult helps with the set up. To prevent tree damage, take down the slackline when finished. Some communities have slacklines set up at local parks. But most slacklines are **portable**, which means they can be brought on vacations or to parties.

Before attempting any tricks on the slackline, make safety a priority. Place crash pads underneath the line to help soften falls. Do not attempt highlining. Highlining is for highly trained athletes only.

portable—easily carried or moved

Slacklining is a great way to get outside and spend time with friends. Take it slow and keep practicing. Soon walking the line will become a natural feeling!

Towels or padded wraps can be used to protect trees from slackline damage.

GLOSSARY

altitude (AL-ti-tood)—how high a place is above sea level or Earth's surface

elastic (ee-LAS-tik)—cord that can stretch out and return to its original size and shape

foundation (foun-DAY-shuhn)—the base or basis of something

momentum (moh-MEN-tuhm)—the amount of force in a moving object determined by the object's mass and speed

portable (POR-tuh-buhl)—easily carried or moved

propel (pruh-PEL)—to push forward

pulley (PUL-ee)—a grooved wheel turned by a rope, belt, or chain that often moves heavy objects

ratchet (RACH-it)—a device allowing motion in only one direction

rigging (RIG-ing)—the system of ropes, cables, and other equipment used to suspend a slackline

simulate (SIM-yuh-layt)—to give the appearance or effect of

spindle (SPIN-duhl)—something shaped or turned like a spindle or on which something turns

tubular (TOO-byuh-lur)—round and hollow, shaped like a tube

variation (vair-ee-AY-shuhn)—something that is slightly different from another thing of the same type

webbing (WEB-ing)—a strong fabric, often used in place of a rope

Read More

Kelley, K.C. *Bungee Jumping.* Extreme Sports. Mankato, MN: The Child's World, 2011.

Killcoyne, Hope Lourie. *Extreme Sports and Their Greatest Competitors*. Inside Sports. New York: Rosen Educational Services, 2015.

Loh-Hagen, Virginia. *Extreme Tightrope.* Nailed It! Ann Arbor, MI: Cherry Lake Publishing, 2016.

Internet Sites

American Trickline
https://www.americantrickline.org/

International Slacklining Association
http://www.slacklineinternational.org/

Red Bull: Slacklining
https://www.redbull.com/us-en/tags/slacklining

INDEX